Little Ducks Go

I Like to Read® books, created by award-winning picture book artists as well as talented newcomers, instill confidence and the joy of reading in new readers.

We want to hear every new reader say, "I like to read!"

———————————————————————

Visit our website for flash cards, activities, and more about the series:
www.holidayhouse.com/ILiketoRead
#ILTR
This book has been tested by an educational expert and determined to be a guided reading level C.

Little Ducks Go

by Emily Arnold McCully

I Like to Read®

HOLIDAY HOUSE • NEW YORK

Copyright © 2014 by Emily Arnold McCully
All Rights Reserved
HOLIDAY HOUSE is registered in the U.S. Patent and Trademark Office.
Printed and bound in October 2020 at Toppan Leefung, DongGuan City, China.
The artwork was created with pen and ink and watercolors.
www.holidayhouse.com
3 5 7 9 10 8 6 4

Library of Congress Cataloging-in-Publication Data
McCully, Emily Arnold, author, illustrator.
Little ducks go / by Emily Arnold McCully. — First edition.
pages cm. — (I like to read)
Summary: Mother Duck is on the run trying
to keep her ducklings safe.
ISBN 978-0-8234-2941-7 (hardcover)
[1. Ducks—Fiction.
2. Animals—Infancy—Fiction.]
I. Title.
PZ7.M478415Lhm 2014
[E]—dc23
2013009559

ISBN 978-0-8234-3300-1 (paperback)
ISBN 978-0-8234-3988-1 (6 x 9 paperback)

Little ducks go.

Look out, little ducks!

Little ducks go.

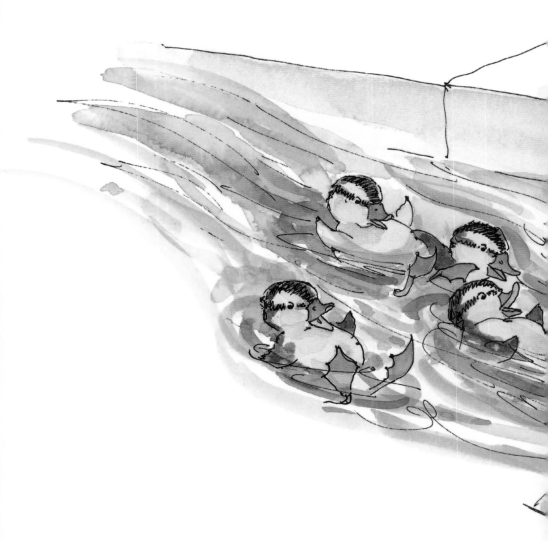

They go down.

Mother looks down.

"Quack," she says.

Little ducks look up.

"Cheep cheep," they say.

Little ducks go.

Mother runs.

Mother looks down.

"Quack!"

Little ducks look up.

"Cheep cheep!"

Little ducks go.

Mother runs.

Cars come.

Look out!

She is safe.

Mother runs.

Little ducks go.

"Cheep cheep!"

Little ducks stop.

Mother stops too.

She wants help.

But the man goes away.

Mother looks down.

"Quack," she says.

"Cheep cheep," she hears.

She sits.

The man comes back.

Little ducks get into the net.

They are safe!

Little ducks go home.
"Cheep cheep cheep
cheep cheep cheep!"
"Quack!"